Chapter 3 – What To Do

When the children met their father, they could hardly contain their excitement. "Puppy, puppy," cried Zachary. "Dad, you have to see this dog! Let's skip dinner and go back to the store!" Matthew suggested. Father couldn't believe his ears. What was going on?

Mom and dad had only recently agreed that it was time to start looking for a puppy. Their family dog, Sasha, was 16 years old. She could no longer hear, and was quite afraid of the two little boys who ran wildly through the house. Her main goal was to stay out of their way! However, buying a dog from a pet store had never been a consideration. Mom and dad believed in adopting homeless pets from local shelters or pet adoption centers. To these animals, adoption could mean the difference between life and death.

Matthew's parents talked with him about pet adoption over chicken nuggets and French fries. Matt asked a lot of questions about shelters and how adoptions work. Mom shared the story of how they adopted Sasha when she was only six weeks old. She also talked about past pets that had been part of the family, all of whom had been rescued. Matthew began to see the difference between buying and adopting. But could they ever find a calm, sweet dog like the Lhasa Apso he had been holding?

   After dinner, it was time to leave the mall. So much for the merry-go-round and Build-a-Bear! Finding a new puppy became the one and only thought in the minds of Matthew and Zachary, and so began the "Adopt-a-Puppy" adventure.

Chapter 4 – The Search

The next morning, Matthew leapt out of bed and bounded down the hallway! Excitement was written all over his face. How he dreamed of caring for his very own dog! He wanted something small, like the Lhasa Apso at the mall, so he could hold its leash by himself. In addition, the puppy must want to cuddle. Finally, it couldn't be too crazy. What kind of puppy would it be? Only time would tell.

First, Matt's father checked the local shelters. He found that most of the dogs were larger than a four year old could handle. He also learned that many shelters have age restrictions and will not allow families with young children to adopt.

Next, his mother looked online. She spent hours scrolling through pictures of puppies and dogs in need of a forever home. But how could they choose from only a picture and sentence or two of description? Puppies have personalities just like people, and it was imperative to find the perfect match.

The following Saturday, the family traveled to three different Pet Smart stores. Every Saturday, these stores hold adoption days in which homeless animals are brought to the stores in hope of finding a family. Matthew and Zachary walked among the cages. A beautiful lab mix caught their attention. With her dazzling eyes and wagging tail, she seemed to say, "Will you play with me?" But she was already too large for the boys to hold.

Next, they saw a poodle mix, but he was six years old and seemed to be shy of children. Though these dogs were very sweet, they weren't the right match for this family.

Matthew started to lose hope. Would he ever find the puppy he longed for? He had so much love to give. Mom and dad told him to be patient. There was one special puppy out there that needed Matthew just as much as Matt needed him. They would continue their detective work until that puppy was found!

Chapter 5 – Surprise!

On Wednesday night after Matthew had gone to sleep, his dad was reading the newspaper.
In the classified section, "Small Puppies Need Home" caught his attention. Could this be the answer?

Quick as a blink, father dialed the number. There were six puppies, three girls and three boys in need of homes. They were 12 weeks old and were expected to be about 15 pounds when fully grown. "How is tomorrow at 11:00AM?" the owner asked. "We'll be there!" father replied.

Thursday morning began like any other day. Matthew woke up, ate breakfast, and played outside in the warm sunshine. All of a sudden, he heard the roar of daddy's truck in the driveway. Beep! Beep! "What are you doing home?" asked Matt. "Today our family is going on a special trip. Climb in!" And off the family drove.

Soon, dad pulled up to a tidy, beige house. "Do you know what is inside, Matthew?" Matt shook his head no. "PUPPIES!" Like a bolt of lightning, Matthew flew out of the truck and up the steps. DING DONG!

Chapter 6 – Matthew's Choice

As the door opened, the sound of puppies floated through the air. "So, I hear you'd like a puppy," the owner said. "I think we may have just what you're looking for!"

Matthew and his family were taken into a small room that looked like a closed-in porch. Soon, the man returned holding puppy number one. This puppy was a little girl with brown and white fur that covered her eyes. She was so cute! Matt stretched his arms out to hold her, but she was a bit wild. The puppy jumped all over Matthew and chomped on his ear. Ouch! Next puppy, please.

Puppy number two looked like a black and white mop. When Matthew held this little boy, the tiny dog snuggled into his lap. It was love at first sight. "This is the one," Matt announced. Mom asked, "Don't you want to see the others? There are four more waiting to meet you." But as mom watched the new friends cuddle on the bench together, she knew there was no need. Matthew had made his choice.

Shortly after, the family traveled home with the newest addition. Since Matthew got to choose the puppy, he promised his mother that she could name him. What was his name going to be? First, mom thought of black and white objects. Piano? How about Oreo? No, Matthew didn't like those names. Then she remembered an adorable little dog she viewed online, whose name was Oliver. Oliver seemed to fit, and she liked the sound of Ollie for a nickname. The family agreed: Oliver it is!

And so, Oliver was on his way to his forever home and Matthew held his new best friend close to his heart.

Edwards Brothers Malloy
Thorofare, NJ USA
July 18, 2012